W9-BRO-279

To the students I met at Indian Hill Elementary who "spoke up" and asked for their names to be printed in my next book: Halima, Zaid.M, Gaby, Mapior, Itzel, Stacy, Stephen, Carlos, Adrian, Jazlynne, and Monica. You are you, and you belong. —M.P.

For all the mean people I've met (and will meet) in my life who've pushed me to speak up for myself, for others, and for what is right. For Chris, who encourages me to speak up. And for you. —E.G.

Clarion Books · 3 Park Avenue, New York, New York 10016

Clarion Books is an imprint of Houghton Mifflin Harcourt Publishing Company.
hmhbooks.com
The illustrations in this book were created digitally using Adobe Photoshop.
The text was set in Sassoon.
Book design by Jessica Handelman
Description: Boston ; New York : Clarion Books, Houghton Mifflin Harcourt, [2020]
Summary: Illustrations and easy-to-read, rhyming text encourage the reader to speak up about everything from their own name being mispronounced to someone bringing a weapon to school. Includes author's note about real people who have found their voices, when to speak up, and how to express oneself without speaking.
LCCN 2019016859
ISBN 9780358140962 (hardcover picture book) · ISBN 9780358136620 (e-book)
Subjects: | CYAC: Stories in rhyme. | Expression—Fiction. | Social action—Fiction. Classification: LCC PZ8.3.P273685 Spe 2020
DDC [E]—dc23
Manufactured in China
SCP 10 9 8 7 6 5 4 3 2
4500802139

SPEAK UP

written by Miranda Paul illustrated by Ebony Glenn

clarion books
houghton mifflin harcourt · boston new york

There are times we should be quiet.
There are days for letting go.
But when matters seem important—

SPEAK UP!

Let others know.

With so many ways to speak up,

like a sign,

a smile,

a shout . . .

if we could make things better,
why not let our words come out?

When you're being introduced
and they get your name all wrong—

SPEAK UP!

Say your name.
You are you—and you belong.

When someone spreads a rumor,
and you're sure it isn't true—

SPEAK UP!

State the facts.
Truth can open up our view.

When a rule just isn't fair
or has gotten much too old—

SPEAK

UP!

Work for change.
Justice comes when we are bold.

When a person wounds another
with their words or with their fist—

SPEAK UP!

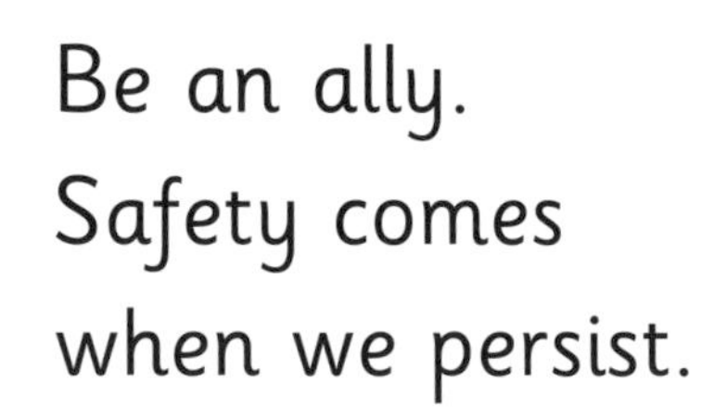

Be an ally.
Safety comes
when we persist.

If you see someone who's lonely,
or they're having a bad day—

SPEAK UP!

Share a moment.
Kindness goes a long,
long way.

When you make a small mistake,
(even if you didn't know)—

SPEAK UP!

Say you're sorry.
Learn to listen. Learn to grow.

When you have a special day,
or you're given something neat—

SPEAK UP!
Shout your thanks.
Gratitude makes life so sweet.

When you're sad or packed with feelings
and the world seems dark and gray—

SPEAK UP!

Ask for help.
Friendship chases
clouds away.

When trees and creatures suffer
from our quick and careless choices—

SPEAK UP!

Rally others.
Nature needs our mindful voices.

When you know a scary secret
about someone getting hurt—

SPEAK UP!

Tell a grownup.
Courage sometimes
means you blurt.

When the group is taking one path
but you know it's not the way—

SPEAK UP!

Change directions.
Leaders don't always obey.

While some people speak up **LOUDLY,**
and your words might whisper *quiet,*
one voice can make a difference,
so don't hesitate . . .

GO TRY IT!

Author's Note

In school, I was mostly a quiet kid. I remember feeling knots in my tummy when I had to talk to grownups or answer questions. I'd clear my throat many times to prevent my voice from cracking. Singing and acting helped me overcome my nervousness and become confident in the power of my voice. As a parent, I've encouraged my children to speak up when things really matter. One day, my son bravely told a teacher about a student who brought a weapon to school. Speaking up allowed his classmates to stay safe. Remember, there are many kinds of communication we can use to help ourselves, others, and our world. One person truly can make a difference.

Peace,

Miranda Paul

Real Kids Who Spoke Up

When they were students, **Hariharan (Hari) Sreenivasan** and **RaKenya (Kenya) Downs** each had teachers who mispronounced their names. Sreenivasan recalls raising his hand and blurting out his name before a substitute teacher had the chance to get it wrong. Downs shortened her first name, but even that led a teacher to make jokes. Both students grew up to become professional journalists who have reported on the importance of pronouncing young people's names correctly. In 2016, they encouraged people of all ages and cultures to share their stories through videos and a hashtag on social media (#ActuallyMyNameIs).

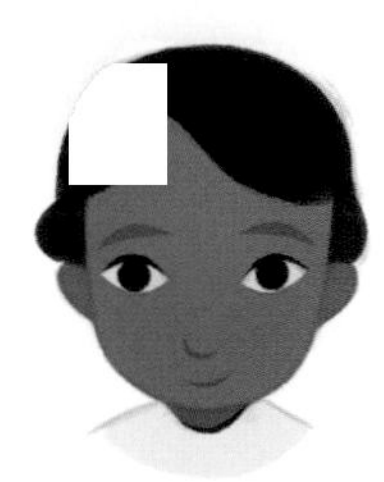

As a young boy, **Thurgood Marshall** debated many topics with his brother and father at the dinner table nearly every night. In high school, he is said to have memorized the United States Constitution, a historical document that explains the rights Americans should enjoy equally. He then became a lawyer and won an important court case that helped change unfair laws that kept black and white students from attending the same schools. After that case, **Ruby Bridges,** at age six, became the first African American child to attend an all-white school in New Orleans, Louisiana. Though people on the sidewalk shouted awful names at her, she didn't miss a day of school during her first year.

Speaking up can be as easy as sitting down! Thanks to **Acacia (Tiny) Woodley** and **Christian Bucks,** recess doesn't feel so lonely for some kids anymore. Woodley, who lives in Florida, designed the Friendship Bench and has traveled around the country to speak about the importance of not leaving anyone out. Bucks, who lives in Pennsylvania, got the idea for the Buddy Bench when he saw something similar at a school in Germany. Now you can find these benches at school playgrounds all over the United States.

Many young people are giving our planet a voice, including **Xiuhtezcatl Martinez,** who has been speaking up about harmful environmental practices at international and local U.S. government meetings since age six and now performs hip-hop songs that call them out. At age twelve, **Param Jaggi** had the idea to invent a filter filled with special algae that attaches to a car and eats up carbon dioxide pollution. By age eighteen, he had started a company to help other kids develop their own eco-friendly inventions. And **Cassandra Lin** was only a fifth grader when she rallied her classmates and started a project to recycle cooking grease into fuel that could heat families' homes in the winter.

When an extremist group called the Taliban took control of the Swat Valley in Pakistan, they demanded rules that banned girls and women from watching TV, shopping, or going to school. **Malala Yousafzai** kept attending school anyway and blogged about her experiences. Then the Taliban shot her! (She's okay now.) Yousafzai continued to speak out and became the youngest person to win a Nobel Peace Prize, inspiring many girls and women to speak up for themselves, and many men and boys to be allies. She's also inspired activists such as **Muzoon Almellehan** to be bold in their efforts to help girls. Shortly after becoming friends with Yousafzai, Almellehan made history, too—she became the youngest Goodwill Ambassador for UNICEF, an important public role that raises awareness about the needs of children worldwide.

When Should You Speak Up?

BE QUIET, LET IT GO	SPEAK UP, LET OTHERS KNOW
Situation is harmless	Someone is hurt or is going to get hurt
Kids can solve the problem	Adult help is needed
Bad behavior is by accident or mistake	Bad behavior is on purpose
You're trying to get someone in trouble	You're trying to get someone out of trouble
Problem can wait to be solved later	Problem is an emergency

Still Finding Your Voice?
Here Are Some Ways to Speak Up—Without Saying a Word!

Make a sign or work of art

Be a witness—record what you see or hear

Attend a march or peaceful demonstration

Refuse to join in negative behavior

Send a thank-you card

Give a gift

Smile or wave

Sign a petition

Write a letter

Cast a vote

Volunteer your time

Donate money or goods

Read books about all kinds of people and experiences

A Special Note: The portraits in the mural the kids are painting are of (left to right): Nelson Mandela, Malala Yousafzai, Martin Luther King, Jr., and Ruth Bader Ginsburg.